Dear Evan,
    It has been a true pleasure to have you in class this year! I have really enjoyed watching you grow and learning about how things work from you! Thank you for sharing your laughter and sense of humor with the class, it brightens the room☺ Also, thank you for your help and dedication in the garden, I hope you come see it in the fall. I know that you will do great next year in 6th grade. You can do it, Evan!
                    ♥Ms. Spaulding

Once I Knew a Spider

To Larry Pringle,
friend and fellow traveler
in the world of books
—J. O. D.

For Devora, Isaac, and Ben
—J. C.

Text copyright © 2002 by Jennifer Owings Dewey
Illustrations copyright © 2002 by Jean Cassels

First published in the United States of America in 2002 by
Walker Publishing Company, Inc.

Published simultaneously in Canada by Fitzhenry and Whiteside, Markham, Ontario L3R 4T8

Library of Congress Cataloging-in-Publication Data

Dewey, Jennifer.
Once I knew a spider / Jennifer Owings Dewey ; illustrations by Jean Cassels.
p.cm.
Summary: An expectant mother watches as an orb weaver spider spins a web, lays her eggs,
and stays with them over the winter.
ISBN 0-8027-8700-2 — ISBN 0-8027-8701-0 (reinforced)
1. Orb weavers—Juvenile Fiction. [1. Orb weavers—Fiction.
2. Spiders—Fiction.] I. Cassels, Jean, ill. II. Title

PZ10.3.D52 On 2002
[E]—dc21
2001026345

The artist used gouache on 140-lb. Arches hot press 100% rag watercolor paper to create the
illustrations for this book.

Book design and composition by Diane Hobbing of SnapHaus Graphics

Printed in Hong Kong

2 4 6 8 10 9 7 5 3 1

Once I Knew a Spider

Jennifer Owings Dewey

Illustrations by Jean Cassels

Walker & Company
New York

It was July, the hottest month of the summer, the time of shimmering blue skies and double rainbows after rain. I was expecting our first child. In the afternoons I rested in the coolness of the house. I placed my favorite rocking chair next to a small window set low in the adobe wall of our bedroom.

One day a spider appeared on the window ledge outside the glass. Right away she began to spin a web.

The spider started with a single silk thread and ended with a graceful construction shaped like a wheel of fine lines fastened together. The inner spiral was composed of sticky silk, while the rest of the web was not sticky.

The colors on the spider's body, her eight slender legs, and the design of her web told us she was a common orb weaver.

She rested when her work was done. She hung upside down at the web's center, her back to the setting sun, as still as if she were dead.

The spider came to life at night. She turned into a light-footed, agile hunter, racing across her web strings to pounce on moths, flies, and grasshoppers.

The spider bit her insect meals with her fangs and paralyzed them with venom. She spun ropes of silk in which she wrapped their bodies. Then she hung them on her web.

The spider always had food around for hungry moments.

I grew bigger with our child, and the spider got bigger, too.
   "Maybe she's going to be a mother," my husband said. "She might lay eggs soon."
   And this is what happened.

One day the round, fat spider dropped from her web to the window ledge. There she spun a tiny napkin of silk.

Upon this she deposited
a cluster of glistening eggs.
Each was the size of a pinhead.

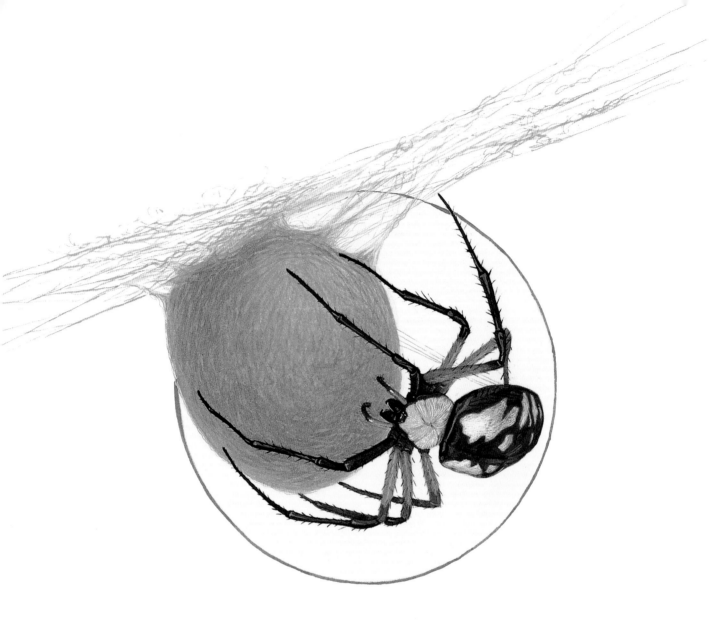

The spider began to spin a sac to surround and protect her eggs. Ribbons of silk poured from her back end while her eight legs worked swiftly to mold and shape a round shelter. The inner layers were of soft, fluffy silk. The final outer layer was tan silk with a waterproof sheen to it.

"You've done a wonderful job," I said to the spider when I saw she was finished. "Your eggs have a yellow rain slicker to grow in."

The spider tucked her sac into the darkest corner of the window frame. Jays, flickers, and magpies darted under the cottonwood trees. Each day ravens flew through the yard. I worried that the spider and her egg sac would become a meal for a hungry bird.

"You've done well to choose this window frame," I said. "The birds fly by too fast to notice you. I'm glad of that, because I like watching you."

The spider was strong after building her egg sac. She thrived on a rich diet of insect prey, creatures that bumbled into her web. When my baby was born in late August, I held her in my lap and told the spider what she was like.

"She has red hair and hazel eyes," I said. "She is very pretty."

Then I held the baby up, young as she was, so the spider might have a good look.

Autumn days were warm, with nights cool enough for sweaters. October frost burned brown spots on the apples still hanging on the trees in the orchard. We wondered how the spider would do as the weather changed.

There were fewer insects for her to capture and eat, but she appeared to be fine.

Then winter blew across the land, and with it came the cold.

One morning we woke up to fresh snow on the ground. I went to the window, expecting to see the spider stiff and frozen in her web. I tapped on the glass and she moved.

"Come see!" I called to my husband. "She's still alive!"

We could hardly believe it. Most orb weavers die when winter comes.

Snow had piled up six inches deep on the
window ledge. Heat from inside the house
warmed the glass enough that a tiny snow cave
formed around the spider.

My husband came to look. He held our baby close and said, "The spider has an igloo of her own to live in."

The spider remained alive. Her egg sac was tucked close against her belly. She ate nothing, so far as we could see.

"Maybe I ought to try and feed her," I suggested. "It's hard to see her getting thinner every day."

"I don't think you can," my husband said. "It's nearly impossible to change nature's plan."

Spring came and the snow cave melted. The spider, shriveled and pale, set to work on a new web. It was half the size of her first but beautiful just the same.

Strung into the fragile strands of her new silken trap was the egg sac, still yellowish and shiny, and safe from harm.

On a morning in June, I sat outside with my baby on my lap. Out of the corner of my eye, I saw a cloud of spiderlings drifting on the breeze.

"The sac opened!" I cried.

Hundreds of spiderlings clung to the window ledge and wriggled their way up the glass. Some tumbled down the side of the house while others took to the air, held aloft by puffs of silk streaming from spinnerets on their back ends.

I found the spider mother curled into a ball, her eight legs tucked close against her belly. Her colors had faded away. She was dead. "You did your job," I whispered to the spider. "You did it well."

Bright early summer days followed. After they hatched, baby spiders drifted and floated everywhere in the yard. Tiny, pale, eight-legged bodies made lacy patterns against the sky. Many spiderlings clung to blades of grass and buds on the trees.

One morning all but a handful disappeared. Those that stayed spun fine, wheel-shaped webs. One infant orb weaver chose the window frame as the site for hers.

None of the spiders survived the next winter, as their mother had. She was different from any spider we ever knew. Her young grew up and built egg sacs of their own, which hatched in the spring, and so their mother's spirit continued on. We are reminded of her each time we see an orb weaver spinning a web in our yard.

Author's Note

The world's spiders have several characteristics they share, which make them different from insects. All spiders have eight legs and two parts to their bodies. All eat meat. Spiders are the only animals on Earth able to make silk their entire lives. Spider silk is produced in glands in a spider's abdomen. The silk flows out through tiny holes called spinnerets.

An observer of spiders will discover that their behavior may vary from one region to another. Cold or hot weather, and other environmental factors, can alter a spider's method of hunting or the site it chooses for a web. Clearly the orb weaver described in this story was an exceptional spider, one that broke the rules by living beyond the usual life span for this type.

Orb weavers spin silk webs that have a circular or oval shape. They are most often found among grasses and weeds in meadows or along streams, places where insects abound. They are sometimes found in windows.

Orb weaver spiderlings emerge from their egg sac in late spring and balloon to new destinations, carried on the wind by single lines of silk trailing from their spinnerets. Most die when winter comes.

Orb weavers, like other spiders, depend on silk, the miraculous fiber made inside their bodies. The silk that comes out of their spinnerets is used for web making, for trapping prey, and for building egg sacs, among other uses. A well-fed spider, one that catches lots of insect prey, will produce more silk than a spider with too little to eat. It is likely the spider in our window survived the winter on nourishment stored in her body. She was a fine hunter, a survivor, and, like all life big and small, she was one of nature's miracles.